K-3

FORKS A 9 6 '85

D0499974

MONTA D 8 24 8?

KLA. R A3 16

E
Wah   56487
c.1   Wahl, Jan

           The Five in the Forest

      Siskiyou County Schools Library
             Yreka, California

THE FIVE
IN
THE FOREST

BY
JAN WAHL

with illustrations by Erik Blegvad

Siskiyou County
& Schools Library

FOLLETT PUBLISHING COMPANY

CHICAGO

Other popular books by Jan Wahl are:

PLEASANT FIELDMOUSE (1964, pictures by Maurice Sendak)
CABBAGE MOON (1965, pictures by Adrienne Adams)
DOCTOR RABBIT (1970, pictures by Peter Parnall)

Text copyright © 1974 by Jan Wahl.
Illustrations copyright © 1974 by Erik Blegvad.
All rights reserved. No portion of this book
may be reproduced in any form without written
permission from the publisher. Manufactured
in the United States of America.

ISBN 0-695-40446-6   Titan binding
ISBN 0-695-80446-4   Trade binding

Library of Congress Catalog Card Number: 73-90051
First Printing

For
my
mother
with
Love

Armida came running to a meadow
where bluebells rang whispering music
and wrens pushed out of brown nests
and violets and cowslips lay.

On the soft wide meadow Armida
started dancing.

Mama and good Baba were far behind,
working in the garden.
She was free to spin and tap her
feet on the enchanted earth.
Dragonflies whirred, but she
could not catch them. Through
the air came the call of a wild,
wild bird.

Armida tripped on something in
the grass, immense and glittery—
an egg of painted glass. Where might
she open it? In a secret place.
She ran to the forest close by.

Into the forest, through golden specks
of light, past grassy places and
grasshoppers' homes. At last she
was alone with the egg. She shook it
slowly, hearing SOMETHING.

Behind her, four solemn rabbits
were approaching.

They walked very stiff and tall.
They saw Armida with their precious
egg, which they had made with
extra care.

Armida did not see them approach.
She was lost in happiness in the
cool green wood. She untied
the egg. Mama seemed
very far away.

The egg was filled with paper grass,
which flew in all directions.
Startled, she lay it on the ground
under a great birch tree.
The rabbits came closer.

Armida heard a sound
like faint thunder.
She twirled, astonished.
"Who are you?" she said.
In the dim-lit wood
the afternoon was
turning blue.

The rabbits laughed aloud.
They explained the egg was theirs,
reaching out eight gentle paws.

"No!" Armida shouted. "It's mine!
I found it!"

"What do you like about it?"
asked one long-eared gentleman.
"It's a beautiful egg," she replied.
"I love it as if it were my own."

"Yes," chimed in the second rabbit.
"It's our favorite one. It protects
the forest from harm.
That is our Egg of Good Luck."

On it were faded painted flowers
and pale designs.
It was snow- and mildew-stained.
"It has been with us a long time,"
the third explained.

They showed her their nest in a secret
hollow, overflowing with painted
eggs. They told her how they
colored them, how they hid them
from the neighbors.

Spinach leaves made green. Yellow
was squeezed from gorse beneath
each heel. Logwood gave the richest
purple dye. Deep scarlet
came from cochineal.

Eggs were shaped from marble,
alabaster, glass, and wood.
Or borrowed from hens.

"But why do you do this?" Armida asked,
glancing over the egg tower.

Ah, they answered, since days
of Old eggs have been hidden—
among the bean blossoms,
in mounds of straw,
in empty shoes,
under pillows.

"We distribute them every Egg Saturday,"
stated the fourth.
"We think it better to hunt for eggs
than otters and weasels or,
A-HEM, rabbits."

Armida listened, and nodded.
She searched for one with her
name printed on it.
But she loved that
glass egg so!

The rabbits crept on soft feet
back to the nest, watching and
guarding their Good Luck Piece.

They gave her a party hat
once found among the fireweeds.
Violet clouds stretched above,
keeping the forest
muffled and private.

"I must get home before moonrise,"
she sighed, studying piled-up eggs.
Suddenly the glass egg moved.
The rabbits gasped.
The egg was rolling!

End over end the egg rolled,
bumping and rattling.
They watched it go,
worriedly wringing
their paws.
"Slow, dear egg!
Slow!"

The two halves parted.
More paper grass flew out.
From out of the inside
a smaller egg
whirred upward.
It floated toward
Armida.

"I was sure *something* was in it!"
Armida clapped her hands,
taking care not to lose
the fancy hat.
Quick as a cat
she caught the wobbling
miniature egg.
Its wings shook,
a bit unsteady.
How she wanted that egg!

36

"An egg in our egg!" sneezed
the rabbits. (Rabbits often sneeze
when they don't understand.)
Armida got ready to depart.

"Wait, I remember!" the third
rabbit roared. "The little egg
was so lovely, I hid it in
the bigger one, long ago,
to keep it safe!
Let's give it to her *now*."

"Splendid!" she sang out.
Before she popped the
party hat back on,
the second rabbit suggested—
"We might have fixed
an awfully nice
nest in your hair."
Her feelings about THAT
were mixed.

They all waved good-bye.
The rabbits gathered a
chain of violets
for her to wear.

Siskiyou County
Schools Library

With a grand *WHOOSH*
the egg carried her high
up above the trees
till the whole forest became
as big as a single leaf.

Armida felt like an eagle
gliding home.
Except eagles
don't live in houses
with blue roofs,
nor with Mamas
and Babas
racing forth to give
a welcoming kiss.

And eagles never
get rushed in to supper
with raspberry pie.
And eagles don't
get to eat with hats on.

Nor do they
bring rabbit eggs
down from the sky.